With ██████████████████████ ones

For Zennor and Izzak Tejani

www.seaquestbooks.co.uk

ORCHARD BOOKS

First published in Great Britain in 2016 by The Watts Publishing Group

1 3 5 7 9 10 8 6 4 2

Text © 2016 Beast Quest Limited.
Cover and inside illustrations by Artful Doodlers with special thanks to Bob and Justin
© Orchard Books 2016

Series created by Beast Quest Limited, London

A CIP catalogue record for this book is available from the British Library.

ISBN 978 1 40834 097 4

Printed and bound by CPI Group (UK) Ltd, Croydon, CR0 4YY

Orchard Books is an imprint of Hachette Children's Group
and published by The Watts Publishing Group Limited,
an Hachette UK company.

www.hachette.co.uk

HYDROR
THE OCEAN HUNTER

BY ADAM BLADE

ORCHARD

>THIS IS DR SHAH, CHIEF BIOLOGIST.
I MUST BE QUICK BEFORE THEY FIND ME.

ALL OUTGOING RADIO MESSAGES ARE
BEING MONITORED, SO I'M SENDING THIS
ON A CODED FREQUENCY.

QUANTIUM-5 IS NOT WHAT IT SEEMS.
IT'S ALL A LIE. THEY'RE BUILDING
SOMETHING HERE. SOMETHING TERRIBLE.
I SHOULD NEVER HAVE BEEN SO FOOLISH.
I TRIED TO REFUSE, BUT NOW THEY HAVE
MY FAMILY. I HAVE NO CHOICE.

WAIT… I HEAR FOOTSTEPS IN THE
CORRIDOR. IF YOU ARE RECEIVING THIS
MESSAGE, WHOEVER YOU ARE, BRING
HELP. TRUST NO ONE.

THEY'RE COMING. I HAVE TO GO. PLEASE
COME. BEFORE IT'S TOO—

[TRANSMISSION ENDS]

STORY 1:

DECEPTION AT QUANTIUM-5

CHAPTER ONE

ABOARD THE BEHEMOTH

"**T**his sub is awesome!" Max said, as he looked round at the glossy black lines and curves of the *Behemoth*'s main corridor. Lights glared down from the metal walls, and reflected brightly in the inky floor. Overhead was an arched glass ceiling. It barely seemed to separate them from the darkness of the deep ocean outside. Lia kept close at Max's elbow, hugging herself and frowning at the walls as if they might close in on her.

"Hmm…" she said.

"Oh, come on!" Max said. "We're on a scientific discovery mission – not getting our teeth pulled out. Try to look a bit more excited."

Max knew the Merryn princess would much rather be swimming free with her swordfish Spike than stuck inside – but still… Max glanced back to check on his pet dogbot, Rivet. At least he seemed happy enough, trotting behind them and sniffing at the recycled air.

Ahead, Max's mother, Niobe, paced slowly beside Councillor Leos, smiling and nodding as they chatted. When they reached a pair of steel doors, Leos drew a key-card from his pocket and swiped it over a sensor. The doors swished open. Max and Lia followed them into another corridor. This one was spotlessly white with a low ceiling and thick

glass walls. Beyond the glass, men and women in white coats peered down microscopes or stared at tanks full of seaweed. Councillor Leos turned to Niobe and pointed through the glass.

"Our scientists are examining a new type of seaweed. We collected it on our last mission to Quantium-5," he said. "It could be a new source of fuel."

Lia leaned close to Max. "I don't know why the old walrus looks so pleased with himself," she whispered. "It's called stink weed. We Merryn use it to keep insects away."

Max looked again at Leos's silver hair and drooping moustache, and choked back a laugh. With his hands held behind his back and his chest puffed out, the councillor definitely looked more than a little walrussy.

Niobe shot Max a warning look and he dropped his grin.

"It is wonderful to have you here," Leos said to Niobe. Then he turned his twinkling blue eyes on Max. "And you, young hero of Aquora. Your insight will be very useful. The gold at Quantium-5 may all be gone, but we're discovering new plants and animals on every trip." Leos beamed down at Lia, showing his straight white teeth. "And having our very own Merryn princess with us is a real honour." The councillor patted Lia's shoulder, and she did her best to smile, though it looked more like a grimace.

Niobe cleared her throat. "It's very exciting to be part of the team."

Max nodded. "Definitely. And I'm looking forward to playing around with the old mining tech. We're glad to be of help, right, Lia?" Lia didn't answer. Max followed her gaze to a huge, dark porthole window. He nudged her with his elbow. "Right, Lia?"

"Hmm? Oh, yeah, sure..." she said. Once Leos and Niobe had started off again, Lia sighed. "I'm missing Spike already," she said.

"You'll be back with him in no time," Max told her. "And Leos might be a bit pompous but he means what he says. Your help really will be very useful."

Max heard a scrabble of metal paws, and looked up to see Rivet sniffing at the base of a heavy steel door ahead.

"What's through there?" Max called, pointing at it.

Leos turned. "Hmm? Oh… Just storage. You know, supplies and what not."

But as they passed the door, Max couldn't help noticing an eye scanner built into the metal. *A bit extreme for a storage room…* he thought. Then he smiled at himself. *This is a scientific discovery mission – not a Sea Quest.*

That's probably just where Leos keeps his moustache wax.

Leos led them onwards through another sliding door, and they entered a large control room. "The bridge," he said, spreading his arms wide. A sleek computer bank ran the full width of the room. Uniformed naval officers sat before it, tapping away and looking at the window at the front of the ship. Beyond the glass, two beams of white light barely

penetrated the murky ocean. Red lines on the glass outlined the invisible seascape all around them. Max saw a silhouette of a shark swim past.

"The tour is finished," Leos said. "Now, there will be a meeting of all our head scientists. Niobe – I'd like you to attend." Leos turned to Max and Lia. "I'm sure you young people would enjoy a little time off." He snapped his finger. "Lieutenant!" Leos called.

A tall, slim man with greased-back hair and a sharp beak of a nose turned to face them. Max's stomach sank.

Lieutenant Jared? You have to be kidding!

Leos put his arms around Max and Lia's shoulders, ushering them forward. "Will you do the honours, Lieutenant?"

Jared flashed Max his familiar, sneering smile. "I would be delighted, Sir!" he said.

Max caught his mother's eye and raised his eyebrows in disbelief. Niobe looked as if she might protest, but Leos quickly steered her away.

"Follow me, children," Jared said, then marched off without a backward glance.

Max and Lia followed him back into the main corridor.

"How on earth is that guy still a naval officer?" Lia hissed.

Max frowned, suddenly feeling worried. Jared had arrested both Max and his father on more than one occasion – not to mention almost starting a war. "The last time I saw him, Jared was in deep trouble with the Aquoran Council," Max whispered. "But it never seems to stick."

"I'm not surprised, with all that grease in his hair," Lia muttered.

Jared stopped before another set of doors.

He swiped his key-card, and a lift opened. As soon as the doors shut behind them, Jared turned to Lia and smirked. "I'm surprised to see you without your breathing mask on," he said. "Why aren't you suffocating? I thought your type couldn't breathe air."

"What do you mean, her type?" Max said. "Lia is a Merryn princess, and you'll treat her with respect!"

"It's all right, Max," Lia said. "Jared's just showing his usual charm." She turned to the lieutenant. "I've eaten some special kelp," she said. "Now I can breathe air just as easily as you." Lia smiled sweetly. "How about I take you for a swim outside later? We'll see how you do without your mask."

Jared scowled and stalked out of the lift. He led them along another white corridor, lined with glossy doors.

A soft beep echoed from above, and a robotic voice spoke through the speakers. *We are approaching Quantium-5. All naval officers to their stations.*

Jared opened a door with a swipe of his card and gestured inside with his thumb. "You kids stay put in your bedrooms," he said.

"No wandering around. I've got important business to attend to." Then he turned on his heel and strutted away.

Max stepped into the suite. It was decked out like a typical Aquoran apartment with a video screen and computer desk. There were three cabins. Rivet bundled past and leapt up onto a plump couch.

"Well, Jared hasn't changed," Lia said, slumping into a chair. Suddenly, she winced and put her hands to her temples. "Ah!"

"What is it?" Max asked. Lia let her hands fall. She shook her head.

"I don't know," she said. "It felt like a sea creature in pain, but I couldn't hear where it was coming from."

"Hmm…" Max frowned. "I'm starting to get a bad feeling about this trip. Firstly, the security seems way over-the-top, then Jared turns up, and now this…" Max crossed to the computer and tapped in his password. The screen flickered into life with the words *Welcome to the Behemoth*, projected in 3D. There were other standard icons for vids, news and games. Max quickly hacked the system. He used his finger to swipe through a load of scientific files and information on the crew. *Nothing of interest there…* He carried on searching the system and found a whole raft of hidden, high-security files. "Bingo," Max said. He opened one called 'Operation Hydror'.

The screen instantly filled with detailed diagrams.

Machine parts, Max realised. He enlarged one, and stared. It looked like some kind of armour. "I knew something was going on!"

Whoop! Whoop! Whoop! A loud siren blurted through the sub. Max jumped. The red words "SECURITY BREACH" flashed across his screen.

"That doesn't sound good!" Lia said. Max quickly shut off the computer.

"GRRRR!" Rivet growled at the door. It slid open and four officers stormed through. They were pointing huge blasters.

"Don't move, and keep your hands where I can see them!" one shouted. A moment later, Jared strode into the room.

"You are all under arrest," he said.

CHAPTER TWO

QUANTIUM-5

A huge officer with a shaved head shoved a blaster in Max's face. Max raised his hands, backing away, but another officer grabbed his shoulder and slapped a pair of handcuffs over his wrists.

"You can't do this!" Max cried. "We're guests, not criminals!"

Jared shrugged. "That's something you'll have to take up with Councillor Leos." A third officer approached Lia, but Rivet growled and bared his metal teeth.

"Call that mutt off before I'm forced to deactivate it," Jared snapped.

Niobe appeared in the doorway behind him.

"What is going on in here?" she demanded, skirting past Jared into the room.

Jared gazed down his nose at Niobe. "Max hacked into our secure systems – we're taking him into custody."

"I was just playing on the computer," Max said. "I didn't know I wasn't allowed."

Jared rolled his eyes at Max. "And I suppose you can't read the word *restricted* either," he said.

"Look!" Niobe said. "I'm a lead scientist on this trip; my husband is Head of Defence in Aquora. Max is a national hero. There shouldn't be any files we can't look at! Jared – I'm well aware of your history. If you don't let Max go, I'm heading straight to Councillor

Leos to find out what you're trying to hide."

Jared glared at Niobe for a long moment, then finally turned to his officers. "Release the boy," he said. As the guard unlocked Max's handcuffs, Jared caught Max's eye. "If I catch you poking about again, there will be trouble!"

The lieutenant gave Niobe one last venomous scowl before heading for the door.

"Ruff!" Rivet let out a loud bark as Jared passed.

The lieutenant jumped a foot into the air. Once he'd recovered, he rounded on Rivet, drawing back his foot.

"I wouldn't do—" Max started, but Jared's kick landed on Rivet's metal side with a clunk. The lieutenant cried out in pain, then limped from the room.

That had to hurt! Max thought.

Jared's four guards marched after him, clearly trying not to laugh.

Once the guards' footsteps had faded, Max closed the door.

"What on Nemos was that all about?" Lia said.

Max shrugged. "I don't know, but it must have something to do with those secret files. Mum – do you know anything about Operation Hydror?

Niobe shook her head. Then she sighed and rubbed a hand over her face. "In fact, after my brief from Leos and his scientists I'm very confused about this trip. Nothing they said seemed right. They waffled on about kelp, but we've been exploring Quantium-5 for decades."

A shudder ran through the sub's walls, and the engine hummed. Max felt the vessel slow.

"We're preparing to dock," he said. Max crossed to a porthole in the far wall and peered out. Sure enough, he could see the old mining colony below them, lit up in the *Behemoth*'s headlights. The colony was a series of tarnished metal domes sitting at the bottom of a deep-sea trench. A few of the domes were built against the trench wall, which rose high above them, out of sight. Nearly all of the round structures were covered in weeds and barnacles. Long tunnels ran between them but many were broken and flooded. Small portholes were lit up like glowing eyes in a few of the bio-domes, showing that some were still in use. Only the largest dome looked in good shape, though, with gleaming metalwork. A thick viewing window ran all the way around it, and Max could see blinking computers and

control panels inside. A long tunnel was extending from the *Behemoth*'s docking bay, towards a door on the dome.

Max noticed old mining tech lying on the sea bed. He felt a surge of excitement. There were huge digging robots with four legs and arms, armoured transport vehicles, and massive cranes and drills.

"Look at all that cool tech!" Max said, pointing.

Lia raised an eyebrow. "Looks a bit rusty."

All personnel to the docking bay, the ship's tannoy echoed from the speakers. *We have reached our destination.*

"Come on, then," Niobe said. She hefted a small backpack over her shoulder and headed towards the door.

Max and Lia followed with Rivet and they joined a line of naval officers filing along the sub's corridors. They marched through a hatch and into a crowded docking bay. No one spoke, and an atmosphere of fear hung over them.

Something strange is definitely going on here, Max thought.

Once everyone was inside, an alarm sounded and the sub doors slid closed behind them. A wide metal door opened ahead, into the bio-dome.

Max, Lia and Niobe shuffled forward with the others. They entered a dimly lit tunnel with Rivet just behind them. Boots rang on the metal grid-work floor. Corroded metal curved around him. Blue lighting in the low ceiling gave everyone's faces a ghostly glow. Dented heating pipes ran across the ceiling. They reached a heavy-looking door. Max noticed the original lock and handle had been removed, and a key-card access panel welded in its place. They stopped as Leos reached into his pocket.

Lia shivered, and rubbed at her arms. Grimy ventilation shafts were belching out freezing air. "This is not quite what I was expecting," she said, under her breath.

Max ran his eyes over the old tech. It was all at least a decade out of date. "Me neither," he whispered.

"Follow me," Leos said, over the humming of the air pumps.

He swiped his key-card and led the group of scientists and officers into a concrete spiral staircase, encased in a metal cage. As they climbed, Lia caught Max's eye and wrinkled her nose. Max nodded. The sharp smell of disinfectant hung in the air, along with the metallic tang of rust.

Finally Max reached the top of the staircase, which led into the control room he had seen from the sub's porthole. He stared round in wonder. Vid screens cycled through views of dimly lit rooms filled with rusting furniture. Rows and rows of switches with red and green lights blinked on the control panel. The sprawling colony of bio-domes could be seen through the panoramic window.

Councillor Leos waited, smiling broadly, while the rest of the passengers assembled before him, shuffling to get a good view.

Finally, when everyone was inside, Leos held up his hand for silence. "Welcome to Quantium-5," he said. "For those of you that have not been here before, I know the run-down state of the mine can be alarming. But I assure you, this bio-dome has been fully updated. You are perfectly safe, as long as you

don't wander out of bounds. I would now like to invite all scientists to a meeting. Please follow Lieutenant Jared. Naval personnel, you know your duties."

The crowd separated in different directions.

"So what are we supposed to do?" Lia whispered.

Before Max could answer, Councillor Leos strode towards them.

"My dear guests!" Leos said heartily. "I hope you are enjoying your trip so far. Niobe – once again, I would like you to attend this meeting. Max and Lia, you are free to make your way to your accommodation – room 6b, on the ground floor of this bio-dome. Please don't stray beyond the main living quarters in the central dome. Much of the facility is in disrepair and many rooms are closed off and without air. Now, Niobe, after you," Leos said. He swept a hand towards the door the other scientists had taken.

Niobe raised an eyebrow to Max, then strode away, followed by Leos. The door slid shut, leaving Max, Lia and Rivet alone – apart from the six armed guards stationed around the walls, anyway.

"This place seriously gives me the creeps," Lia muttered.

"Smells funny, Max," Rivet barked.

"I'm with you on that, Riv," Max said, keeping his voice low so as not to be heard by the guards. "There is clearly something going on in here that's got nothing to do with kelp. Something Jared doesn't want us to know about. And you know what that means?" Max said.

Lia smiled. "We're going to find out what it is!" she said.

CHAPTER THREE
OUT OF BOUNDS

Max, Lia and Rivet slipped away from the guards. They clattered back down the winding staircase, all the way to ground level. They found themselves in another wide hallway with the same grid-work floor and the same noisy ventilation pipes whirring overhead. Corridors marked with room numbers led off from it. Max peered down the first passageway, and caught sight of a white-clad scientist using a key-card to slip through a newly secured door.

"There are so many locks in here!" he said.

Lia nodded, frowning. "It's almost as if they think their seaweed samples are going to grow legs and walk away!" she said.

Max led Lia and Rivet past the entrances, avoiding guards and scientists. They stopped at a heavy metal door. A huge red sign hung above it, glowing in the dim light. *Restricted Access.*

Max turned to Lia and grinned. "That looks more like it!" he said.

"Apart from the fact it's clearly locked." Lia said.

"Someone coming, Max," Rivet barked.

Max listened, and heard the clang of booted feet from the stairwell behind them, along with the low rumble of men's voices.

"This way!" he said, darting for the cover of a metal pillar.

Lia and Rivet ducked behind him, just

as a pair of guards strolled into view. The men looked quite old. They were balding and carried some extra weight around their stomachs. But their muscled arms still looked powerful, and their gloved hands rested on huge blasters slung across their chests.

"I'd kill for a cuppa right about now," Max heard one man say.

"One more patrol of the base, and our shift will be over," said the other.

"About time!" said the first. "Dull as dishwater down here. Last time I volunteer for a secret mission, that's all I'm saying."

Secret mission? Max held his breath and put a finger to his lips as the two men marched past, straight towards the doorway marked *Restricted Access.*

"Be ready," Max whispered.

One of the guards swiped his card and the huge door slid open.

"Now!" Max said.

He, Lia and Rivet darted after the guards, the sound of their footsteps drowned out by the whir of the air recycling system. They dived through. The tunnel door slid shut behind them. Max and Lia clung to the wall with Rivet, hardly daring to breathe until the guards were out of sight.

Max grinned. "Time to explore!" he said.

They followed the dark metal tunnel, careful not to catch up with the guards. They reached a small bio-dome with an ancient-looking computer desk and filing cabinet in the centre. Scraps of browning paper were scattered over a dusty concrete floor. Doors to more tunnels led off in every direction. Rusted bolts that didn't look like they'd been moved in years secured most of the doors, but two stood open.

"Which way did the guards go, Riv?" Max asked.

Rivet sniffed at the concrete for a moment, then pointed towards a tunnel with his nose.

"Then we'll go the other way!"

Max led Lia and Rivet through the second tunnel and into another small dome, lit by a single dangling bulb, and packed with piles of crates and boxes. Max read the faded label on one box and wrinkled his nose.

"Beans," he said. "Six years out of date. These must be supplies for the mining colony. Let's keep going, see if we can discover more."

Max, Lia and Rivet filed past the crates into another tunnel. It led into a grimy dome filled with tables and benches. A strip light on the ceiling buzzed and flickered. Piles of trays sat beside a serving hatch in a partition wall. Off to one side, Max spotted a dusty hover-ball table.

"The canteen, I guess," Max said. "This place is eerie. Like a prison, or a ghost town."

"I don't like it one bit," Lia said. She glanced about at the tarnished walls.

They passed through more domes filled with old tables, rusted bedframes and stacks of chairs, shoved together for storage. One dome contained nothing but tiered metal shelves piled with hard hats and folded overalls. Each time, a new tunnel led them onwards, until a final passage ended in darkness. Chilly air wafted out towards them. It stank of engine grease. Max ran his fingers down the wall beside the tunnel entrance, and felt a bank of switches. He turned them on one by one. Vast floodlights in the ceiling blinked into life, lighting up a huge half-dome built against the trench wall. The floor was bare rock.

An old digging dome! Max realised. Holes had been dug in the trench wall, and some were covered by metal bars. Goosebumps prickled Max's neck. *They're almost like prison cells*, he thought. Then his eyes fell on piles of abandoned tech.

"Whoa!" Max said. "This is almost as cool as the tech graveyard in Sumara!" Hover transporters, cranes, drills, carts… Every bit of mining tech Max could think of crowded the space. A long window in the metal wall overlooked the colony behind them, and Max could see the control-room window lit up brightly in the distance. Uniformed officers gazed out through the glass. Max ducked into the shadow of a huge drill.

"Try to keep out of sight!" he told Lia and Rivet. Max ran his eyes over the tech and

spotted something that made his skin tingle with excitement. "No way!"

A huge, five-metre-high robotic suit stood near the trench wall. Apart from a crack across the giant bubble-shaped helmet, it looked in good shape. Bright yellow paint and reflective strips covered the metalwork. Massive legs with hydraulic joints ended

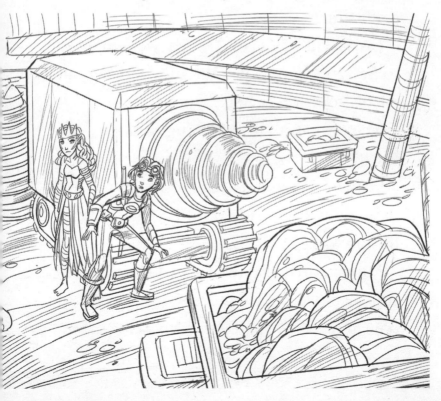

in flipper-feet with built-in thrusters. One colossal arm wielded a broad shovel in place of a hand, while the other had a two-pronged claw. Rivet bounded over to the robot, tail wagging.

"Big roboman play, Max?" Rivet barked.

Max grinned. "I think that can be arranged, Riv," he said, making his way towards the giant suit.

Lia rolled her eyes. "Aren't we supposed to be keeping out of sight and working out what's going on in here?" she said.

Max shrugged. "If that thing works, we can use it to help us."

"How?" Lia asked. "Are you going to hit Jared with that spade until he tells us what he's up to?"

Max ignored Lia and flipped open Rivet's storage panel. *Some opportunities are just too cool to pass up...* He took his screwdriver, then scrambled up the hand and foot holds that led to the robot's cockpit and climbed in. He sat in the padded chair surrounded by buttons and levers. The glass helmet gave him a 360-degree view.

Max hit the power button. Nothing happened, so he unscrewed the control panel. Underneath, he found some chips and wires covered in black gunk from a leak. Max made some tweaks, bypassing the corroded circuits, then flipped the panel shut. *That should do it!* Sure enough, when he hit the power button, the lights on the control panel blinked on. *Cool!* Max tugged at a lever, sending the robot's shovel arm swinging downwards.

"Watch out," Lia cried, as the metal spade swished past her, far closer than Max had intended.

"Sorry!" Max called. He spotted a small

box attached to the robot-suit's helmet, with a sensor pointing through the visor. *Remote scanner*, Max read. He'd heard of remote scanning tech before, used for dangerous industrial work. *Hmm...*

Max climbed down from the robot's cockpit, and stood in front of the towering metal suit.

"Scan me!" Max said. A red beam of light

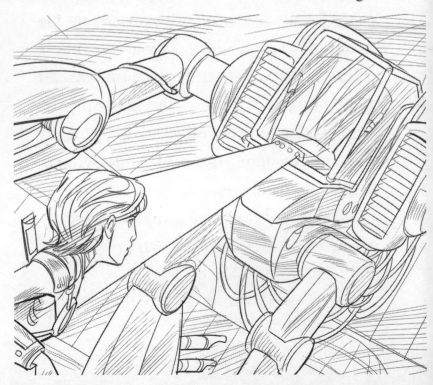

shot from the scanner, zipped up and down Max's body, then blinked off. *Cool!*

"Now, activate remote control mode," Max said.

The scanner light flashed once in reply. Max lifted his arm carefully, remembering how close he'd come to swatting Lia. The robot's arm jerked upwards, mirroring his movement.

"Yes!" Max said. At the same moment, Lia let out a yelp of pain. Max turned to see her double over, her hands clamped to the sides of her head, and her eyes squeezed shut.

"Lia! What is it?" he asked.

Lia slowly unbent, her whole body shaking.

"There's an animal in serious trouble nearby." Lia gasped. "We have to help it!"

CHAPTER FOUR

A TERRIBLE SECRET

Max hurried after Lia, picking his way carefully between the rusted hulks of drills and cranes. Rivet padded behind them. Max's robotic suit screeched and clanked as it followed them across the dome, mirroring Max. Finally Lia stopped beside a shiny new metal door, double-bolted and secured with an eye-scanner. She was sweating a little.

"Something's trapped behind there!" she said.

"Stand back," Max told Lia and Rivet. He

rapped twice on the door with his knuckles.

Lia rolled her eyes. "Like knocking's going to—"

Boom! A vast metal spade slammed into the door above Lia's head, denting the metal. Max's robot suit swung again. *CRASH!* The metal buckled, the bolts snapped and the door flew open with a bang.

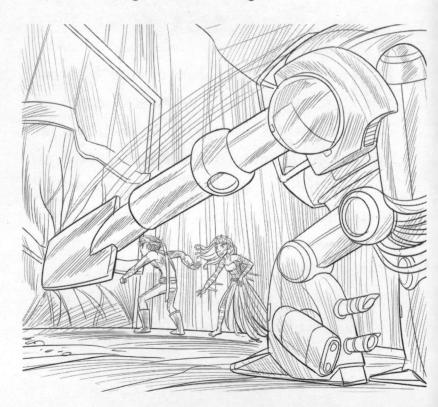

Max grinned. "Cool, huh?"

Lia looked pale. "Warn me before you do that again."

Through the door, Max could see a bright, modern workshop built in one of the domes. There were benches loaded with bits of tech. Max stared closer, and all the excitement drained out of him in an instant.

"Deactivate remote control," Max told his robot, his stomach churning with dread. Then he drew his hyperblade, gritted his teeth and stepped through the buckled door with Rivet and Lia behind him.

Huge diagrams of robotic tails, jaws and armour plates covered the workshop walls. Metal models sat on benches beneath the diagrams. Max gasped.

"They're designs of Robobeasts," Max said. He recognised parts from many Robobeasts he'd faced on Sea Quests – Fliktor's tongue,

Brux's armour plates, Tengal's jaws, complete with deadly circular saws. Every vile, twisted weapon Siborg and the Professor had ever created lay before him.

Max shook his head with horror. "This is no scientific research lab," he said, his throat dry. "This is a weapons research facility!"

A low, trumpeting moan filled the room. Lia stepped forward, eyes wide. The sound came from behind a pair of metal doors dividing the lab. Max raced towards them and hit the release button. What he saw inside sickened him to the core. Lia let out a cry of dismay and Rivet growled. A glass vat of water dominated the room. Cranes and ladders ran up the side, and a platform strewn with metal plates, electric screwdrivers and welding tools spanned the top.

Inside, a dark shape thrashed and twisted, frantically swooping then diving, leaving a trail of glimmering bubbles in its wake. Max caught glimpses of a torpedo-shaped body, a pale grey underbelly speckled with black dots and a long-flippered tail chained to the floor. *A leopard seal*, Max realised, but it was the biggest he'd ever seen – at least as long as a hoverbus. The creature swooped past, and its dark eyes met Max's for an instant. In their inky depths, Max saw an anguish and terror so strong it made him catch his breath.

The seal shot upwards, straining its chain to the very limit. It just managed to thrust its whiskered snout out of the water and snatch a gasp of air, before being tugged back into the depths of its tank.

Lia raced to the tank. "What have they done to you!" she cried. Then she turned to Max. "I'll try to calm it."

She closed her eyes and turned back to the panicked creature, muttering some soft words

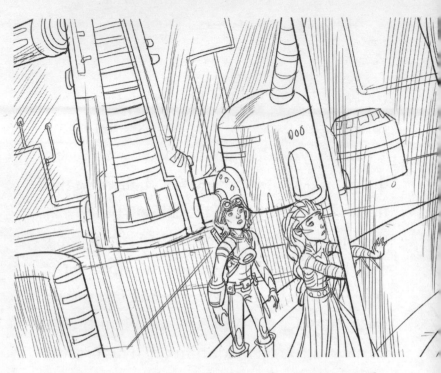

in Merryn. The seal slowed momentarily, and Max noticed circular scars and scabs on the creature's speckled skin. Each puncture mark filled him with disgust.

I never thought I'd see the day when Aquora harmed innocent sea creatures.

Lia turned to Max, wringing her hands. "We have to get it out of there," she said. "The pain is driving it mad."

Max crossed to a vid screen built into the

side of the tank. A diagram of the seal's prison and surrounding machinery revolved slowly before him. Max drew his fingers across the screen, zooming in on what looked like an exit shaft built into the base of the tank. It led out to the open ocean.

"Got it!" Max said. "I just need to activate the release…" He hit a red button, and a whirring sound echoed from beneath the floor, then a clank. The metal cuff that held the seal's tail sprang open, and the bottom of the tank slid away, revealing a funnel-shaped opening sloping into darkness. A terrific gurgling filled the room, and the water in the tank quickly spiralled away. Max caught one last look at the seal's dark eyes before the creature was flushed out into the sea.

Max and Lia raced to a porthole and looked out into the dim waters.

"There!" Lia cried, pointing to a sleek silhouette. The seal spiralled upwards before dipping its nose and swimming a neat loop-the-loop. The sight made Max's chest swell.

"It's thanking us!" Lia said, but then she gave a gasp. "No!"

Max's throat tightened in horror as white beams of light criss-crossed the water around the freed creature. A pair of Aquoran subs swerved into its path, releasing red streaks of blaster fire. The seal flicked its tail and darted upwards, heading towards the distant surface, slaloming through the sizzling blasts.

"Ahh!" Lia cried as a red beam struck the seal's chest. Its body jerked, and its tail thrashed with pain. The subs knifed towards it. Through their watershields, Max could see Aquoran officers, bent over the controls, their eyes fixed on the injured animal.

"Seal hurt!" Rivet barked.

"We have to help it!" Lia cried.

Max was already halfway across the room. He clambered up a metal ladder with Lia right behind him. Together they stepped out onto the platform above the tank. Max glanced down into the shallow water at the bottom, then turned to Lia. She nodded. They bent their knees and leapt.

Max hit the water and slid down a narrow tube before he shot out into the sea. Lia was at his side in an instant. Above, Max saw the lead sub fire a net, which tangled around the seal. It thrashed its tail as the sub drew it in.

I can't let them capture it again!

Max kicked his legs and swam towards the trapped seal. He grabbed the net with one hand and drew his hyperblade. The seal bucked as Max hacked at the metal wires, slicing through one, then another. Soon he'd made a hole. But the seal's flippers were tangled so tight it couldn't escape. Lia drew back her spear and jabbed the sharp tip into the metal fibres that trapped a front flipper. The seal writhed, and Max almost lost his grip. He clung tight, slicing another wire.

Suddenly, white light surrounded him, hurting his eyes. He turned, squinting into the brightness. An open net, like a web with weights at the corners, filled his view.

Before he could move, heavy metal ropes struck his chest, arms and legs, wrapping around him. They held him tight. He was tugged through the water, towards a sleek black sub. Through the sub's watershield, Max caught sight of Jared's gloating smile.

"No!" Lia shouted.

Max twisted back to see a net close around her too. They were both trapped.

We've failed.

CHAPTER FIVE

PRISONERS!

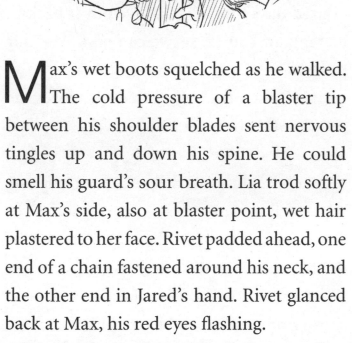

Max's wet boots squelched as he walked. The cold pressure of a blaster tip between his shoulder blades sent nervous tingles up and down his spine. He could smell his guard's sour breath. Lia trod softly at Max's side, also at blaster point, wet hair plastered to her face. Rivet padded ahead, one end of a chain fastened around his neck, and the other end in Jared's hand. Rivet glanced back at Max, his red eyes flashing.

"Trapped, Max!" Rivet barked.

"Get a move on, you stupid mutt!" Jared growled, jerking the chain.

"Gently!" Max snapped. Inside he was fuming, his mind filled with thoughts of the trapped seal. He couldn't believe the evil his own people were capable of. "Jared, what did you do to that seal?" he shouted.

Jared didn't look back. "We put it back in its tank, of course, so we can complete our project."

"But it's wrong!" Max cried. "It makes the people of Aquora as bad as every criminal we've ever defeated."

Jared simply yanked Rivet's lead, tugging the dogbot onwards. After a series of corridors and tunnels, they came to a set of double doors. Jared swiped his key-card over a sensor, and tugged Rivet inside. Max felt a shove from behind and he and Lia stumbled on after Rivet.

Max glanced about, recognising the huge half-sphere of the drilling dome, filled with tech and backed by the trench wall. They'd come a different route – but it was just as they had left it, except that the door leading to Hydror's tank had already been replaced.

Max heard Lia gasp. She pointed towards one of the cage-like openings in the trench wall ahead. A pale face looked back at him from the darkness behind the bars. Max recognised it with an electric shock of alarm.

"Mum!" he shouted. Niobe nodded, her lips tight and her eyes blazing with fury. Max turned to Jared. "What have you done?" he growled.

Jared smiled, showing his rat-like teeth. "We had to build those cells after a few of our scientists wouldn't complete their work." he said. Then his smile changed to a vicious scowl. "I always knew your meddling would get you into trouble, Max. Now you're going to rot down here at the bottom of the ocean with your mother." Jared glanced at the guard behind Max. "Show our guests to their room," he said.

Max felt the blaster dig deep into his back. He started forwards with Lia at his side. One of the guards took hold of Rivet's chain. Max, Lia and Rivet were herded towards the jail cell. Max's mind raced, looking for a way to escape, but his blaster and blade had been confiscated. A young, dark-haired soldier unlocked the door to the cell. Max felt a heavy boot in the base of his spine and fell forwards. Niobe reached out a hand, steadying him. Max turned to see Lia and Rivet shoved into the cell behind him. The door slammed shut. Jared flashed Max one last victorious smirk, then walked away, followed by his guards.

"Thank goodness you're safe!" Niobe said.

"But what are you doing in here?" Max asked her.

"They wanted me to work on their project," Niobe said, louder now the guards were out of earshot. "Torturing a captured seal to make a Robobeast. All that rubbish about seaweed is just a cover story to get the best scientific

minds to come and work here. We're told the truth when we arrive, but by then it's too late. If we refuse to work, we're thrown into cells. Apparently someone tried to get a message out to the Aquoran Council and since then they've only got more ruthless."

"But Leos is on the council!" Max said. "He can't know what's really going on here!"

"Oh, on the contrary." A low, smooth voice spoke from nearby.

Max turned to see Councillor Leos pacing towards them. A white-coated scientist scurried at his side, her dark eyes troubled and her slender arms loaded with blankets. Jared strode behind them.

Leos stopped before the cage door and his blue eyes glittered. "This is all my operation," he said.

"How could you?" Max cried in shock. "Surely the rest of the council can't know what you're doing?"

Leos sighed. "Alas, most Aquorans are far too short-sighted to understand the threats we face, or what we must do to protect our people. Only a very few of us know the details of this operation."

"But you can't hurt innocent sea creatures!" Lia cried.

Leos gave a small shrug. "I have no choice," he said. "It is my duty to protect Aquora. What is one seal weighed against the safety of thousands of innocent women and children?"

"It means everything," Max said. "It's what keeps us a nation of honest, decent people, instead of evil criminals!"

The councillor's blue eyes iced over. "I wouldn't expect a child like you to understand," Leos said. Then he raised a silver eyebrow at Niobe. "An educated scientist like yourself is a different matter altogether, though. Now you've had time to think through my plans, I expect your full compliance."

"Never!" Niobe said. "You've lost your mind if you think you're doing this for Aquora. You're doing it for power. I'll never help you!"

Leos shook his head and let out a heavy sigh. "What a shame..." He turned to Jared, who was practically quivering with anticipation. "It looks like Niobe needs to be persuaded," Leos said.

"Guards!" Jared cried.

Two men stepped forward. Max recognised the older guards he and Lia had followed from the main dome – one had thinning hair combed over his head, while the other was almost bald with a plump face. Max leapt in front of Lia and his mother, fists raised.

"Don't touch them!" he said. At his feet, Rivet growled.

"Don't worry, young man," Leos said calmly, as the bearded guard unlocked the door. "It's you we're after."

The guard grabbed Max's wrists and tugged him from the cell. Rivet snarled.

"No!" Niobe cried.

"Leave him alone!" Lia shouted.

Max heard the scuff of their boots behind him, but Jared lifted his blaster and pointed it at Max's head.

"Stay where you are," Jared told Niobe. "Or it will be my duty to blow your boy's brains out."

Jared took something from his pocket that looked very like a metal dog collar, then stepped towards Max, grinning. He lifted the collar, moving closer so his face was only inches from Max's. Max could see every greasy bristle on Jared's thin moustache. He tried to back away, but strong hands held him still. Jared reached round and snapped the collar shut around his neck.

Max's guard bundled him back into the cell. Councillor Leos drew a small gadget from his pocket and held it up.

A remote control, Max realised.

"Max's collar holds explosives," Leos said,

his eyes on Niobe. "Once I press this button, Max will have ten seconds left to live."

Max felt a wave of hot terror flood through him. Niobe's face turned almost grey.

Leos glanced at Max. "Don't attempt to take it off," he said. "It will detonate if anyone tries. Care to reconsider, Niobe?"

"But I don't even know how to make a Robobeast!" Niobe cried.

The councillor held up the controller, his thumb hovering over the red button. Max's muscles tensed in fear. Leos glared at Niobe.

"You are Aquora's most talented scientist. You will complete Hydror, or Max will die."

Niobe bowed her head and closed her eyes. She drew a deep breath. When she looked up, she seemed totally defeated.

"Don't help him, Mum!" Max said.

Niobe smiled sadly. "I have to," she said. Then she nodded to Leos.

The two old guards took hold of Niobe and led her from the room. Fury burned in Max's belly as he watched her go.

Leos let out another loud sigh. "Believe me, Max, it pains me to have to treat you this way, but I need your mother's help, and I can't allow you to leave Quantium-5." Then he turned and followed Niobe from the room.

Jared remained behind, as did the scientist he and Leos had arrived with. Jared jerked his thumb towards Max's cell.

"Go on then, Dr Shah," he said. "If you will insist on taking care of the prisoners."

The doctor hurried forward and pushed a pair of blankets through the cell bars, followed by some packets of food and a flask of water.

"I'm so sorry," she said in a whisper. "We have no choice. If we don't help, they go after

our families." Then she stepped away.

"Oh, just one more thing," Jared said, pushing past her, one hand hidden behind his back. He lunged at Max, brandishing a stun blaster.

Crack! Blue light sizzled through Max's brain, then darkness closed around him.

CHAPTER SIX

SONIC BOOM

"**P**repare for weapons testing!"

Max jolted upright, the words echoing through his mind. He leaned back against the cell wall, trying to focus his eyes.

"Wake up, Max!" Rivet barked, nuzzling Max's shoulder.

"It's all right, Riv," Max said, patting his dogbot – although the pain in his head was blinding.

Beside Max, Lia sat up slowly, rubbing her eyes. "Did I hear something about weapons testing?" she asked, her face pinched with worry.

Max put a hand to the metal collar at his neck, and a jolt of fear sizzled through him. "Mum must have helped them finish Hydror," he said.

"Um, I think we've got an audience, Max," Lia said, pointing.

Max followed the line of her finger, and peered out through the long window that spanned the curved metal wall ahead. Past a stretch of dusky ocean, Max could see the control room of the main colony bio-dome, lit up brightly, and figures watching from behind its vast viewing screen.

Max squinted and picked out Leos. The councillor stood gazing out through the inky water, a team of scientists at his back. Beside Leos was Max's mother, gripped by guards.

A flicker of movement in the water above

the window caught Max's eye. A dark shadow passed across it.

"What is that?" Lia asked, her voice low.

Max stared into the dark waters, then gasped. A sleek, speckled body swam into view – the huge leopard seal from the tank, but horribly altered.

The creature's dark eyes stared out from holes in a bulky metal helmet that covered its whiskered snout, leaving its sharp teeth free. Breathing tubes ran from the helmet, passing over its nose to its cheeks. More armour plates covered its chest and tail. A small box on the side of the seal's helmet blinked with a red light. Max felt sick.

"Leos has really done it," he said.

Lia nodded, her eyes filled with sorrow. "He's turned that poor seal into a Robobeast."

The speaker above Max let out a belch of static, then Leos's voice came through.

"Hydror, target the drilling bio-dome."

The seal flicked its armoured tail, and turned in the water until its inky eyes seemed to stare straight into Max's own. The memory of Councillor Leos's words echoed hollowly in Max's mind.

I can't allow you to leave Quantium-5…

"They're testing Hydror on us," Max said, realising what was happening.

"Sealbot coming, Max!" Rivet barked, his red eyes fixed on the window.

Beside Max, Lia shuddered. "I can feel its thoughts," she said. "Full of pain and anger. And hunger. It hasn't eaten for weeks."

"Great," Max said. "We're being served up like a tin of tuna." He swallowed hard. "Riv, can you bite through these bars?"

"Try, Max," Rivet barked. He clamped his teeth around a metal strut.

Max kept his eyes on Hydror gliding slowly towards them. The sound of Rivet's teeth grating on metal echoed through the bio-dome.

"What do you think it's going to do?" Lia asked. Max shook his head.

"I can't see any blasters, but there has to be something…"

Hydror stopped, just metres from the drilling dome window. Beyond the

Robobeast, Max could see Leos in the main dome, craned forwards, staring through the glass at his creation.

Rivet let go of the bar. "Can't do it, Max!" he barked.

Max cursed softly under his breath. "If only we still had my hyperblade."

"Or my spear," Lia said. "Or even one of those fancy key-cards."

"Of course!" Max said, glancing at the key-card reader welded to the door. He knelt and flipped open Rivet's storage panel. Max grabbed his screwdriver, leapt up, and unscrewed the back of the reader.

"Hurry!" Lia said. "The seal's doing something!"

Max glanced at Hydror, just outside the window. The creature's throat seemed to be inflating, bulging outwards...starting to quiver. Max turned back to the panel. He tinkered with some wiring.

"Try the door!" Max told Lia.

She pushed the bars, but the door didn't budge. Instead, the whole bio-dome seemed to shudder. Max and Lia clapped their hands over their ears as a low trill rose and fell around them, getting louder and louder.

Outside the dome, vibrations rippled along the blubber of Hydror's throat. Max could see a haze of movement in the water all around it. The drilling machinery in the dome started to rattle in time with the strange, trumpeting sound. The floor shook, and the walls of the dome trembled like a struck gong.

"Leopard seals have immensely powerful calls," Lia shouted, in a voice full of panic. "And that one is bigger and stronger than any I've seen."

Leos has turned that seal into a sonic

weapon! Max realised, as metal clanked and clattered around him.

A crack, loud and sharp like splitting ice, sent a stab of fear along Max's spine. A jagged line appeared in the glass window of the drilling dome.

"Get out, Max!" Rivet barked.

Max gritted his teeth and studied the card reader again. It was a mass of tangled wires, but he yanked two loose.

This had better work.

He touched the bare ends together. With a click, the door swung open. Another crack echoed around the dome, and Max looked up to see the long window ahead shatter and cave inwards, followed by a torrent of white, foaming water.

BOOM! Another crash filled the dome, followed by the hideous groan of bending metal.

"Hydror's smashing the place to pieces!" Lia cried. "We have to get out before we're crushed."

"Run!" Max cried.

Lia, Max and Rivet burst from their prison. Sea water rushed towards them, lapping around their shins. Max slipped then stumbled up again. He heard the wave slap against the trench wall behind them as he splashed through the flow. The tide swirled, rising higher, soaking Max to the waist.

Time to swim!

Max kicked towards the broken window, fighting against the fierce current. Lia quickly took the lead, swimming hard and fast on the surface.

"Here, Riv!" Max cried.

The dogbot paddled to his side. Max grabbed Rivet's metal back and clung on. Rivet tugged Max towards the window.

Already, Max could hear grating creaks from all around them, loud over the rush of water. Each of Hydror's blows added to the scream of tearing metal as the structure around them gave way. The water now lapped above the level of the broken window. Lia dived, and Rivet ducked after her, pulling

Max beneath the surface.

Lia's hair flowed silver behind her as Max swam after her. Huge chunks of twisted metal plunged into the water around them, sending up clouds of bubbles. Max's heart

beat like a drum in his chest. The current snatched the breath from his gills. Rivet's engines whirred…

Finally, Rivet tugged Max through the broken window and out into the open ocean above the mining colony. Max drew a long breath of relief over his gills, but then almost choked on it. Hydror was just ahead, eyes filled with rage, and toothy jaws spread wide. Beyond the captured seal, Max could see Councillor Leos through the window of the control dome. Beside Leos, Niobe covered her mouth with her hands, her eyes round with horror.

Leos's lips moved and the tinny words came over loud speakers, distorted by the water. "Kill them!"

Max saw the red light on Hydror's control box blink in time with the command. Hydror's head came up, and his dark eyes flashed with menace. The seal flicked its tail and powered towards them.

CHAPTER SEVEN

DRIVEN TO DESTROY

Hydror rippled through the water with effortless grace. Max pointed towards the trench wall behind them.

"Split up and head for a cave," he cried, hoping to buy them time.

Lia sped away. Rivet's motors whirred as he tugged Max towards the cliff-face. Max glanced back to see Hydror angle after Lia. The Merryn princess kicked her legs and dived into a narrow crack in the chasm wall.

She's safe! Max thought with relief, trying to find a gap for himself. "Hurry, Riv!" he cried.

A rumbling boom drowned out his words. Max glanced sideways to see Hydror strike its massive armoured head against the rock face right above Lia's hiding place. Chunks of rock rained down the cliff and silt billowed up.

"Help Lia, Max!" Rivet barked, slowing.

Hydror cannoned into the rock once more.

NO! Lia will be crushed! Max scanned the old mining equipment scattered along the base of the trench wall. A huge crane with a massive wrecking ball swinging at the end caught his eye. "That way, Riv," Max pointed.

Rivet angled downwards towards the crane. Max leapt though the crane window and into the driver's seat. Boom after boom rang out from the cliff face above them.

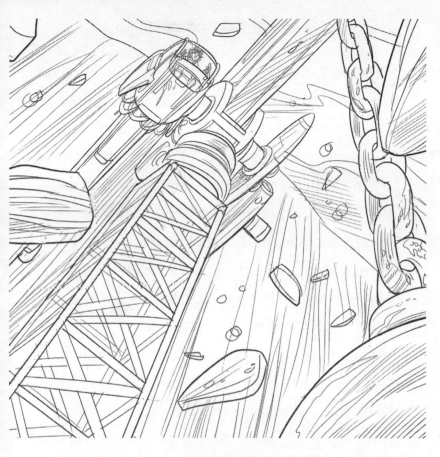

Max hit the ignition. The crane's engine
spluttered and choked, but then started up
with a whirr. He took hold of the steering
and tugged. The crane turned with a jolting
lurch, almost throwing Max from his seat.

BOOM! Max looked up and his chest
tightened with fear – a great crack gaped in

the rock above Lia's cave.

"Get out of there, Lia!" Max shouted. "The cliff's going to give way!"

Lia slipped from her hiding place just as the whole rock-section collapsed, swallowing her in a cloud of silt. For a second, Max's stomach melted with terror. Then he saw her emerge safely through the falling rubble... right in Hydror's path!

She's trapped! Max yanked at the lever for the crane arm. It swerved to one side, the long chain dragging the wrecking ball in a long, sweeping arc.

The Robobeast hovered in front of Lia, watching her hungrily. Max recognised the look of a predator savouring the moment before the kill.

Max pulled back on a lever, turning the crane and bringing the wrecking ball swinging back the other way...

Lia screamed and flung her arms up to protect her face as Hydror knifed towards her...

CLANG! The wrecking ball ploughed into Hydror's side, smashing the blinking control box and throwing the great seal sideways just as its teeth slammed shut. Lia let her arms fall and opened her eyes. Max shot from the crane window.

"That way, Lia!" he called, pointing at a hefty boulder on the seabed.

Lia dived towards it. Max and Rivet met her halfway. Together they kicked behind the boulder, and looked out.

In the dark water by the trench wall they could see Hydror writhing and twisting, thrashing its head and tail.

"What's it doing?" Max asked. "The control box has been destroyed."

Lia put her hands to her head and focussed

on the struggling creature.

"No one is controlling it now. It's trying to get free of that armour. I tried to tell it to stay calm and we'll help, but it's in too much pain to listen."

"Hydror, find that boy and the Merryn girl!" Leos's tinny voice screeched through the colony's tannoy. "Devour them!"

Hydror's massive body froze. Then the seal turned slowly in the water until its eyes fell on the bright window of the control room in the main bio-dome. The creature opened its colossal mouth and roared. Max and Lia threw their hands over their ears, watching as Hydror's trumpeting bellow blasted the dome, making it shudder. Councillor Leos

stared open-mouthed, while the scientists behind him all flinched. Hydror's roar fell silent. Max watched, horrified, as the huge seal edged closer to the window.

"I said kill them!" Leos bellowed.

BOOF! Hydror's huge head struck the bio-dome window. *Crash!* Its tail slammed into the reinforced plexiglass. Max heard cries of alarm over the speakers.

Hydror backed slowly away from the window. The creature's massive throat bulged and started to quiver. A long, shuddering note filled the ocean, so loud Max could feel it deep in his chest. Even Rivet hid his head under his metal paws.

The main bio-dome shook as if it had been struck by an earthquake. Through the window, Max saw Niobe and her guards stagger. Several of the scientists lurched and fell. Then the lights inside the dome flickered and went out, replaced by an eerie red glow.

"All that painful tech is sending the seal wild with fury," Lia said. "It wants to destroy the colony and everyone inside. We have to remove the armour."

"I might be able to prise it off if I had my hyperblade," Max said, racking his brain for a solution. "But even that would be tricky."

The seal's bellowing call stopped abruptly. Max watched the furious creature swoop upwards, towards the docking tunnel. Its eyes were fixed on the row of small subs that had captured it. *Crunch!* Hydror's tail smashed the first away into the ocean. *SMASH!* Another sub fell away, battered almost flat. Then, with a frenzied series of monstrous blows, the seal attacked the *Behemoth*, smashing off rudders, propellers and finally the entire engine compartment.

When nothing but torn and battered metal

was left, the seal let out one last furious bellow, then turned and swam away, disappearing into the darkness of the ocean.

Lia let out a shuddering sigh. "The main bio-dome held!" she said. "Your mum is safe."

"For now," Max said. "But all the subs are destroyed. Everyone without gills is trapped. And who knows what Leos is capable of now

his plan is in ruins. Not to mention the fact that Hydror is sure to come back. We'd better head inside."

Max felt at the collar round his neck, and cold fear squirmed in his stomach. If they came across Leos, the councillor would be close enough to detonate the collar and blow Max to pieces.

I have to help Mum and the scientists, Max thought, gathering his courage. *Otherwise they're all doomed.*

STORY 2:

COUNTDOWN TO DEATH

CHAPTER ONE

COWARDICE AND TREACHERY

Max led Lia and Rivet up over the curved side of the main bio-dome to the battered docking tunnel. Most of the airlocks had been damaged, but a couple stood open where the small subs had been smashed away by Hydror's furious attack. The dim red light inside showed they had switched to backup power, but they looked more or less operational.

"In here," Max told Lia and Rivet,

pointing at the nearest airlock.

They slipped inside, and Max hit a red button on the wall. The door closed behind them, and Max flipped a switch to activate the pumps. Once the water had drained away, the interior door slid open. Max peered through into shadowy silence. The rushing roar of the air recycling system had gone.

"Dark, Max," Rivet barked.

The cool blue strip lights had gone out too, each replaced by a faint red glow.

"The whole colony's on battery backup power," Max said. "The main power generator must be out."

Max, Lia and Rivet ran through the metal docking tunnel, and into the dank gloom of the entrance hall. Max crossed to the door Leos had led them through on their arrival, took his screwdriver from Rivet's storage compartment and slid the tip between the door and its frame.

"With the power down, the lock will be out," Max muttered. "So this should open easily enough…" Max jimmied the door open a crack, then pushed it the rest of the way with his hands. "So far, so good!" he said.

Max, Lia and Rivet followed the curved tunnel in the half-darkness, then climbed the spiral staircase to the control room.

As they neared the top, the sound of arguing voices echoed down towards them. "I tell you, everything is under control," Leos's polished voice rose above the rest.

"Yeah, right!" Lia muttered.

Max picked up his pace, his stomach a tight knot of fury. He, Lia and Rivet burst into the room.

Niobe sat in a chair near the control desk, still held in the grip of her guards. At least twenty other guards and scientists pressed close around Councillor Leos. He stood at the back of the room, his hands raised for calm. Jared stood nearby, a film of sweat beading his forehead. As Jared's eyes fell on Max and Lia, they narrowed.

"Seize the prisoners!" Jared cried, pointing.

"No!" a soft female voice piped up. Dr Shah, the dark-haired scientist who had given Max and Lia blankets, stepped out before the crowd. "Don't listen to him," she said. "Leos

is acting against the wishes of Aquora. Just look what his experiment has led to! Unless we do something to get the power back up, we're all going to die!"

"Silence!" Leos shouted. "Dr Shah! You should remember—"

"She's right," Niobe cut through the councillor's words. "Hydror's flooded the generators – we've got about half an hour's oxygen left. Max is an engineer. He's one of

the few people that might be able to save your skins."

Mutters of alarm rippled through the crowd as guards and scientists turned to each other, wide-eyed with fear.

"Arrest them at once!" Jared screamed. "I am your commanding officer!"

The two veteran guards holding Niobe exchanged a glance and nodded. They let go of Niobe's arms and turned their massive blasters on Jared.

"No offence, Lieutenant," the one with thinning hair said. "But I plan to get out of here alive. I think we'll take over from here." He nodded to one of the younger guards – dark-haired and muscle-bound. "Seize him," he said. Jared looked as if he might explode, but before he could find the words to protest, the burly young officer stormed across the room. Jared drew his blaster and aimed it at the young man's chest, his hand shaking and his eyes wild.

"Drop it, Lieutenant," the older officer growled. He and his colleague both turned their blasters on Jared too. He scowled, but let his weapon fall.

Rivet suddenly barked. Max looked to see Leos dart towards a small doorway in the curved wall beside him.

"He's going for the only escape pod!" Dr Shah cried. "We have to stop him!"

The plump-faced guard turned his blaster back on Leos, but the councillor lifted a keypad in his hand. Max's body flushed hot, then cold as he recognised the control for his explosive collar.

"Let me go or I'll blow the boy's head off," Leos said.

Everyone in the room froze.

"Leos," Niobe said. She was trying to sound calm, but Max could hear the strain in her voice. "We need that pod to go for help. Communications are down and all the other subs are destroyed. If you go, everyone here will die."

Leos wrinkled his nose. "Yes, I'm afraid

that is rather the plan," he said. "I can't very well have you reporting back to Aquora, can I? Dear me no, I would be branded a traitor, and that wouldn't suit me at all. So in fact, I'm going to need you all to die, in here or at the teeth of that seal. It's all the same to me."

The councillor turned the handle, and the door opened, revealing a small airlock

holding a one-man sub. As Leos stepped inside, he held up his keypad, and pressed the red button. The door swung shut, and Max felt the collar at his throat buzz. *Beep!*

Ten seconds to detonation, said an electronic voice.

"Mum! Help!" Max cried, grabbing the collar at his throat. Niobe darted to his side.

9… 8…

"You have to stop it!" Lia cried. Rivet whined.

7… 6… Max felt Niobe's cool fingers against his skin as she examined the collar. They were shaking.

"It's wired to blow up if I take it off or stop the countdown!" she said, her voice cracking.

3… 2…

"Then stand back!" Max shouted, pushing Niobe away, horror flooding through him. *This is it! I'm going to die.*

"No!" Lia cried. She covered her eyes with her hands.

Max closed his eyes and held his breath. *BEEEP!* Nothing happened. Max heard Niobe let out a sigh and opened his eyes.

"What happened?" Max said.

"Ahem…" Jared held up his hand, showing a control pad identical to Leos's. "I deactivated the collar. You can take it off now. No need to thank me, it was the only right thing to do."

"You… you… treacherous, stupid, snivelling coward!" Lia shouted. Her face was as pale as chalk, and she looked like she might be sick. "You could have done that before you gave us all a heart attack. You're just trying to save your own skin."

Niobe gently unclipped the collar from Max's neck. Max could see that she was trembling all over.

"No," Jared said. "Leos made me work for him too – honestly. I thought it was terrible the way he was treating Max, I—"

Niobe stormed across the room towards Jared, her jaw clenched and her eyes glinting with rage. Jared cringed against the control desk as Niobe drew back her hand. *SLAP!* A red handprint bloomed on Jared's cheek were Niobe had hit him.

"Shut up!" she said. "Stop trying to worm your way out of this. Of course, I'm grateful to you for saving Max, but it's quite clear you only did it to stop us from feeding you to Hydror like you deserve!"

Jared blinked back at her. Behind him, Max saw the glint of headlights through the plexiglass window, and his belly boiled with rage. Leos's sub hovered outside the window. Inside, the councillor smiled and waved at him through the watershield, before finally banking around towards the open ocean.

"We have to get that pod back!" Max shouted. "Councillor Leos is leaving everyone here to die!"

CHAPTER TWO

HYDROR'S REVENGE

Max watched the pod turn slowly away from the dome.

If only I could disable the sub somehow… he thought. Then he had an idea. He snatched up his collar, and raced to the chamber Leos had used to escape.

Max opened the airlock, threw the collar inside and slammed the door. He tapped a command into a keypad beside the airlock, setting it to launch. Then he turned to look through the window.

A moment later, the collar shot into view, heading straight towards Leos's sub.

Max snatched the control pad from Jared's hand and hit the red button.

"What are you doing?" Jared cried.

"Stopping Leos, of course," Max said.

The collar glowed red as it gained on the sub. Max counted down the seconds in his head. *10, 9, 8, 7, 6... Yes!* The collar looked close enough to the sub's tailfin to do some damage.

BANG! A flash of red followed by a cloud of bubbles and soot exploded from the collar. Leos's sub leapt forwards, then slowed to a stop, trailing a stream of black smoke.

"Good shot!" Lia said.

"Great thinking, Max," Jared cried. "I couldn't have come up with a better…"

Niobe gave the lieutenant a warning look,

and he trailed off. She turned to two young guards. "Put on deepsuits and fetch the pod. Max and I can fix it," she said.

Jared winced. "I'm afraid Leos asked me to pack the deepsuits into his escape sub…" he said.

"And you *did* it?" Niobe shouted. "What kind of idiot are you?"

"Um…I'm not sure you're going to get the chance to retrieve the sub anyway," Lia said, pointing through the window.

A murmur of fear ran through the crowd of scientists, and some backed away from the viewing screen.

Max could see a sleek shape powering head-on through the darkness towards Leos's sub with the speed and power of a hovertrain.

Crash! Hydror's metal snout slammed into the vessel, smashing the watershield like the shell of an egg. Max winced. Several of the scientists in the room gasped. *BOOF!* Hydror struck again, slamming its tail into the pod. Leos shot from the cockpit window into the water, arms and legs flailing. Hydror's dark eyes flashed. Its vast jaws opened wide, showing rows of sharp triangular teeth.

Max saw a trail of bubbles escape from Leos's open mouth as the councillor let out

a silent scream. Then with one strike, Hydror shot forwards and snapped his jaws shut, swallowing Leos whole. The huge seal flicked its tail and swam away.

A terrible hush fell over the room. Max realised he was gripping the back of a chair so hard his fingers hurt. He let go, and took a deep breath.

"Well, that's the end of Councillor Leos," Lia said cheerfully, breaking the stunned silence.

Max swallowed a sick feeling, and nodded. "Unfortunately, it's also the end of our chance of getting a message to Aquora," he said.

"Not quite," Jared said fearfully. "I think I know a way to restart the power."

Niobe scowled at Jared. "Do you really expect us ever to trust you again?" she said.

Jared held up his hands as if expecting another slap.

"No, really," he said. "I've seen the error of

my ways." Niobe raised her eyebrows and met Jared's wide-eyed look with a long, hard stare. "All right," Jared said, finally. "There is another reason. You might not have noticed, but unlike you, I'm not part fish. And dying slowly of suffocation is kind of a nightmare of mine."

Niobe nodded. "That's more plausible," she said. "So, what's the plan?"

Jared sighed. "In a small room off the old miners' canteen, there's a backup generator. Unless it's already flooded, someone can head down and switch over the supply."

Max remembered the grimy bio-dome full of tables and benches they'd passed through when first exploring the base. "I know where that is!" he said. "Lia and I will go. We can breathe underwater, so even if the connecting tunnels are flooded, we'll still make it."

Niobe nodded. "I'll stay here and keep an

eye on Lieutenant 'I'll do anything to save my own skin' over there. Once the power's up, I'll contact Aquora. Good luck," she said.

"Rivet come too!" Rivet barked.

"Of course!" Max said. "We wouldn't be able to see much without you. Set your snout lamp to full beam and stay close."

Max, Lia and Rivet raced from the room and clattered down the dark stairwell until they reached the ground floor. Max levered the tunnel doors at the end of the hall open, and he, Lia and Rivet hurried through the red-tinged darkness. They traced their path back through dusty, disused bio-domes, until they reached the canteen.

"Right," Lia said, once they were inside. "Where's that generator?"

Rivet padded through the room, and the red glow of his nose light fell on a stout metal door by the kitchen.

"Let's try through there," Max said.

He prised the door open with his screwdriver. Inside, they found a huge cylindrical generator half embedded in concrete with the bio-dome wall curving behind it, and pipes and wires running overhead.

"Are you sure that thing's safe?" Lia asked.

"Um…" Max took in the flaking beige paint, rusted bolts and rickety-looking pipes running from the generator to the ceiling. The red beam of Rivet's nose lamp fell on a sticker on the side of the generator. It showed a picture of a stick man being hit by an electricity bolt, beside the word DANGER.

"Probably not," Max said. "But we have to give it a try."

He ran his eyes over a bank of dials and levers beside the generator. All the instructions had worn away, but one huge lever stood out from the rest. Max gripped it with both hands, tensed his muscles, and pulled. The rusted lever shifted with a screech. The generator hummed into life, and the blue lights overhead flickered on.

"You did it!" Lia said.

Max felt the fuggy atmosphere stir as the air recycling system coughed and wheezed into life. He let out a whoop. But then Lia gasped and pressed her hands to the sides of her head.

"What is it?" Max said.

A hollow, metallic scraping sound rang out around them, coming from the other side of the curved wall. It sounded horribly like the screech of armour against the bio-dome. Rivet let out a whimper, glancing up at the metal walls.

"Hydror's here," Lia hissed. "He's just outside. And he's really, really angry."

CHAPTER THREE

THIRTY MINUTES AND COUNTING

Hydror's mighty bellow echoed through the wall, shaking the room. The walls trembled and the pipes on the ceiling jangled and clanked.

"Run!" Max shouted, but he couldn't hear his own voice – and he couldn't move, anyway. Vibrations from the floor climbed his legs, rattling his bones. Cracks opened up all around him.

Hydror's terrible cry rose, until bolts rattled loose in the walls and ceiling, and fell around Max. Pipes screeched as they buckled and fell. Spurts of water shot from between metal plates.

Finally Hydror's call drew to a wavering close. Max staggered to his feet.

"Run!" he told Lia again.

BOOM! The imprint of Hydror's massive

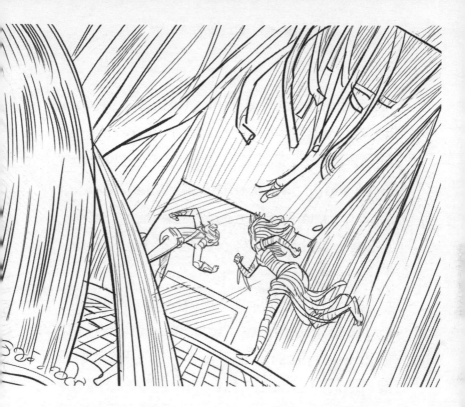

snout smashed out from the wall behind
her, busting the metal panels apart. A rush
of water poured into the room. Something
exploded with a white flash and then the
lights in the ceiling went out.

Max and Lia raced back into the canteen.
Water gushed through holes in the ceiling,
flooding the floor. Their feet splashed as they
ran across the room.

As they reached the tunnel, another *BOOM* rang out. Max saw the corrugated ceiling of the passage collapse, and Hydror's metal snout poked through. Water flooded in, washing away more metal panels.

"Brace yourself!" Max cried as the remains of the tunnel were swept away.

A wave of water hit him, snatching him up. He kicked out of the dome and into the shadowy depths of the open ocean. Rivet and Lia sped to his side. Max pointed towards the main bio-dome.

"That way! Into an airlock."

He grabbed Rivet's back. The dogbot's propellers whirred as he powered away. Lia swam hard and fast beside them, heading for the docking tunnel.

Max glanced back, and terror knifed through his guts. Hydror's eyes were black pits in the darkness, but its white teeth gleamed. Despite the metal covering its body, the creature moved with impossible speed.

The dogbot's engine screamed, running at full capacity. Max fixed his eyes on an airlock. Lia reached it first and dived inside. Max and Rivet flew in after her. Max turned to see Hydror's massive mouth looming towards them, filling the view through the door. He hit the button to close the airlock and held his breath.

Thud! Hydror's huge head crashed into the door as it closed, denting the metal. The water drained out of the airlock. Even before all the water was gone, Max hit the button for the inner door. He and Rivet tumbled through.

They set off at a run, and didn't stop until they reached the command centre. Max leant on his knees to catch his breath, and Lia sank to the ground. Guards and scientists were seated gloomily around the room, all apart from Jared's old grey guard, who still held the lieutenant at blaster point. Niobe sat at the control panel, frantically toggling switches and pushing buttons. Finally, she turned to Max.

"The power's out again," she said. "And this time there's no way to restart it. I did manage

to get a message to Aquora before the power failed. But with only half an hour of oxygen, help will never get here in time."

"So, what do we do?" Max asked.

Niobe took a deep breath. "I took a look at a map of the colony while the power was up," she said. "There are huge ballast tanks under this dome, full of water. If we blow them, they will fill with air and it will shoot us to the surface. The only problem is, the switch to blow them is outside, under the dome. Someone's going to have to go out there."

Max and Lia exchanged a look.

"Not again!" Lia said. "We only just managed to escape Hydror last time. He's way too quick. If only Spike were here! He could outrun Hydror any day!" Lia's eyes lit up suddenly, as if she'd had an idea. She put her hands to the sides of her head, and gazed out into the water beyond the viewing screen.

As Max stared into the ocean beside Lia, a cluster of pulsing electric blue lights appeared in the darkness. Max could just make out a translucent jelly body around them, and long, coiling tentacles.

"A giant squid?" Max said. "It's very pretty, but how is it going to help us defeat Hydror?"

"I was hoping for a sailfish," Lia admitted. "But Ginni is a bluefire squid, and they're pretty fast too. She says she's happy to give me a ride. Ginni and I will distract Hydror while you and Niobe blow the ballast tanks."

Max grinned. "You know what, Lia?" he said. "I think that just might work!"

CHAPTER FOUR

A DANGEROUS DANCE

Max, Niobe and Lia stood side by side. They were in a small airlock chamber, their eyes on the doors leading out into the ocean.

"Ready?" Niobe asked, her words loud in Max's headset, and her hand resting on the blaster in her belt. "Once we're out there, we'll have to act fast. Hydror will be waiting."

Max gulped and wished Rivet was with them – in open water Max would be a sitting duck without his dogbot's propellers. But Rivet's lights would draw the seal in an instant. Max lifted his hyperblade, which Jared had returned.

"Ready," he said.

Lia brandished her spear. "Me too!" she said.

"Then let's go!"

Niobe hit the button for the airlock doors. The doors slid open, and water flooded in. Max drew it over his gills, but clung to the doorframe beside his mother. Lia's friendly squid sped past, the blue lights on her body glittering like stars in the darkness. Lia dived out of the airlock and swooped up onto Ginni's back. She gave Max and Niobe a wave, then shot away through the water. A moment later, the dark torpedo shape of Hydror rocketed after her.

Max and Niobe kicked their legs,

swimming down over the side of the bio-
dome towards the seabed. Max's skin
prickled all over as he swam. The picture
of the massive seal swallowing Leos kept
appearing in his mind. Max shook it away.

I have to focus…

Max and Niobe reached the bottom of
the massive dome. Max saw two enormous

cylinders supporting the giant structure.

The ballast tanks!

"They're filled with water," Niobe said. "Each has a lever on the side. Once we pull them, the water will fire out, replaced with air. The whole dome should float to the surface – or that's the theory, anyway."

"Hurry up, guys!" Lia's voice came loud and breathy through Max's headset. "We can't dodge Hydror for ever!"

All Max could make out of Lia and her squid was a cluster of bright blue lights, zooming through the darkness. Hydror was a blot of deeper black, hot on their tail, climbing and swooping, banking and diving, in a mesmeric dance of death.

"We're on it, Lia!" Max said.

Then he and Niobe swam into the space beneath the dome. It was almost pitch black, overshadowed by the massive structure

above. Without the Merryn Touch, which had given him gills and better eyesight underwater, Max knew he wouldn't have been able to see in the dim water at all. He made his way to the nearest of the two cylinders and looked for a lever. Niobe swam on, heading for the second tank.

Finally, Max found it, attached to the side. The lever was heavily rusted and the rubber grip was cracked. Doubt churned in his belly. The lever looked designed for more than one person to pull, and the rust was sure to have jammed up the hinge.

I can do this! he told himself.

He shoved his hyperblade into his belt, then took hold of the lever with both hands.

"I'm ready!" he told Niobe.

"Me too, Max," Niobe said. "Now, on a count of three. One… Two… Three!"

Max braced his feet against the side of the ballast tank, held his breath and tugged at the lever. It didn't budge. Max tugged again, using every fibre of strength he had. He could feel his muscles screaming. His pulse beat loud in his ears and his arm bones felt like they were bending. Through his headset, he could hear Niobe grunting with effort.

The lever finally shifted, and with one huge effort, Max jammed it down with a screech of metal. Max heard an echoing metallic scream though his headset, and Niobe gasped.

"Done it!" she said. "Now, hold on, Max!"

Max gripped tight to his lever. Beside him, a groan echoed through the tank, followed by a bubbling, glugging sound. A powerful jet of water spurted out from the tank, as the canister filled with air.

Whoosh!

Max shot upwards, pulled by the bio-dome. He glanced down to see the seabed plunging away. Water sped past him, snatching the breath from his gills. His arms felt like they might be tugged from their sockets at any moment. Soon Max could see the dark bio-domes of the colony spread out below. The towering wall of the trench stopped abruptly, replaced by a level plane of rock.

Max saw a pulsing light from the corner of his eye and looked to see Lia speeding towards him on Ginni. But there was no sign of Hydror.

"Look out below, Max!" Lia cried.

Max glanced down to see the seal swooping up towards him. The creature's massive jaws hung open. Its black eyes shone with mindless rage. Adrenaline surged through Max's body. He could see every detail of the seal's tight, constricting armour, and the scars that marred its skin.

Max let go of the lever and threw himself sideways, straight into the jet of water shooting from the ballast tank. The force of the water hit him like a hovercar. It filled his eyes and gills, his mouth and nose, pushing him downwards through the water, away from Hydror's jaws. Finally, Max swam, weak and breathless, out from the dizzying stream. He kicked his arms and legs, righting himself, and looked up to see Hydror smash head first into the base of the bio-dome. *BOOM!* The weaker metal at the base of the structure buckled and split. Hydror shook its massive head and swam away, but Max could see the damaged was done. The bio-dome was already slowing and starting to tip over.

"The dome's taking on water!" Niobe cried.

Max felt a wave of dread as he thought of all the people trapped inside.

They're going to drown!

CHAPTER FIVE

TEAMWORK

Max could see the huge dome above him leaning horribly. Bubbles poured out through the jagged hole torn in its base.

"Are you all right in there, Dr Shah?" Niobe called into her headset.

"We have a few cuts and scrapes, but no one is seriously injured," Dr Shah said. Alongside her voice, Max could hear whimpers and yelps from inside the dome as well as Rivet's worried barking. "The hull is breached, though," Dr Shah said. "I can hear water coming in!"

"Keep everyone calm," Niobe told the doctor. "Close all doors and block any gaps as best you can. We'll get you to the surface."

Niobe swam to Max's side, and Lia swooped towards them on Ginni. Max looked again at the stricken dome and shook his head. He muted his headset so only Niobe and Lia could hear him.

"The dome is rising too slowly," Max said. "We need to get it to the surface before water reaches the control room or everyone will drown."

"Okay, but how?" Lia said.

Max turned his gaze downwards, to the remains of the mining colony below. A smooth circle at the centre, surrounded by broken tunnels, showed where the main bio-dome had stood. Even the red glow of the backup lights had vanished from the portholes of the smaller domes, and the drilling dome lay in ruins.

"There's so much tech down there. Surely there must be something we can use…" Max looked again at the buckled and twisted remains of the mining bio-dome, and had an idea.

"Mum," Max said. "There's a huge robot suit down there with jets. I think I can use it to bring the main dome to the surface."

"Do it," Niobe said. "Lia and I will keep a look out for Hydror and cover your back."

Lia shifted forwards on Ginni's back, and Niobe swam up behind her. Ginni's long, glittering body filled the water.

"Good luck!" Lia called as the squid flexed her tentacles and shot away.

Max took one last look at the listing dome above him. It seemed to be barely rising at all now. Max kicked his legs and swam, angling down towards the damaged roof of the mining dome. A black shadow streaked up towards him.

Hydror!

"We've seen him, Max!" Lia said, speaking into his headset.

The pulsing lights of Ginni's body flitted across Max's path. Hydror changed course in an instant, zooming after the bright squid with her two riders.

The sight of the giant, furious Robobeast trailing his mother and Lia made Max hesitate.

"Please hurry!" Dr Shah's voice came loud and sharp through his headset. "The water's reached the control room. It's coming in fast!"

"Don't worry!" Max answered. "I won't let you down."

Max quickened his stroke, and swam onwards until he reached a huge hole in

the tarnished roof of the drilling dome. He slipped through.

Inside, plates of twisted metal, fallen cranes and broken plexiglass lay in dark piles across the floor. The trench wall threw everything into even deeper shadow. Max strained his eyes, staring about in desperation, looking for any sign of the robotic suit. He spotted a flash of reflective yellow. *Yes!* The robotic suit stood unharmed, near the trench wall, more or less where he and Lia had left it. Max sped towards it, and swam up into the cockpit.

He flicked the power switch, grabbed the steering yoke, then put his foot down hard on the thruster pedal, activating the jets in the feet of the suit.

Vroom! The mining suit rocketed upwards, pushing Max down into his seat and leaving his stomach way behind. It shot out through the broken ceiling of the dome into open water. Max could see the massive main dome floating above him.

"Is everyone okay, Dr Shah?" he called.

"Hurry, Max!" she answered. "We're almost up to our necks!"

Max put his foot down even harder.

Whoosh! The force on his body was tremendous as he powered upwards towards the base of the dome. At the very last moment, he hit the brakes. His stomach flipped at the sudden change in speed, but he toggled a switch, magnetising the robot's metal arms. Clang! Both arms hit the base of the bio-dome and stuck there.

Here goes! Max thought. He slammed his foot down on the thruster pedal. At first he couldn't feel any motion at all, but gradually the dome started to rise. Max willed the robotic suit to keep going, hoping the old technology wouldn't fail.

A streak of bright blue zipped past below him, followed closely by Hydror's sinuous shape. Max saw a steak of red blaster fire ricochet off Hydror's armour.

"Don't worry, Max!" Niobe called. "We're keeping Hydror busy!"

Finally, after what seemed like forever but could only have been minutes, Max noticed the water growing lighter around him. Beyond the base of the dome, he could see

slanting rays of sunshine piercing the gloom.

"We're almost there, Dr Shah," he called into his headset.

Max pushed the thruster pedal all the way

down, giving the dome one last final shove.

"You've done it, Max!" Dr Shah cried, her voice filled with relief. "We're on the surface. And just in time too. I'm evacuating the control room. It's flooded."

Soon Max could see figures bobbing in the bright water beyond the base of the dome.

"Mum! Lia! We've done it," Max called into his headset. "Everyone's safe!"

"Max! We've lost Hydror!" Niobe shouted urgently. "We think he's headed your way!"

Max looked down, and fear fizzed through his veins. Hydror's sleek armoured form glinted in a shaft of sunlight as the mighty seal angled upwards, knifing towards the people treading water on the surface. It was going to rip them apart!

CHAPTER SIX
ROBOT BATTLE

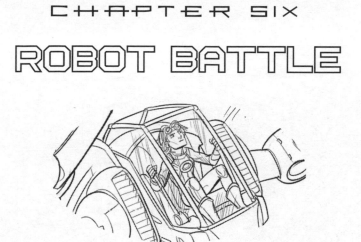

Max disengaged his robot-suit's magnets and jammed the steering yoke forwards. Water whooshed past his helmet as he powered straight ahead. Hydror opened its massive jaws, swooping up towards the group of scientists and naval officers. Max couldn't let them die! He toggled a lever as he neared the seal, drawing back the suit's massive spade hand.

SMASH! Max slammed the spade into Hydror's side, knocking the creature off

course. Hydror shook his giant head, then spun in the water to face Max.

"Are you okay, Max?" Niobe called.

"I've found Hydror," he said, looking into the creature's inky eyes. "You and Lia protect the people on the surface. I'm going to see what I can do about all this armour."

Max slammed the robotic suit into reverse,

shooting away from the Robobeast. *SMACK!* Max's head snapped forwards and he bit his tongue, tasting blood.

I've hit something!

He glanced back to see the curved metal wall of the main bio-dome. Without the robot holding it up, it was fast sinking below the waves. Hydror let out a bellow of rage, drew back its armoured tail, then thrashed it towards Max.

Max thrust a lever forwards, throwing his robot's broad spade hand into the path of the blow.

BOOM! The impact almost threw Max from his seat. He grabbed another lever, sending his robot's huge claw hand towards the armour on Hydror's speckled belly. Max gave the lever a flick. The mining suit's claw grabbed hold of the armour plate. With a twist, he tugged it free.

Thin trails of blood drifted from circular wounds on Hydror's skin. The massive creature shook its head and let out a roar of pain.

CRACK! Hydror's tail slammed into the robot-suit's helmet, jolting Max in his seat and smashing the weakened shield. Water rushed into the cockpit and black dots filled Max's vision. Hydror drew its tail back for another strike. Max jabbed out the claw and snatched Hydror's tail, holding it fast.

Hydror bucked and twisted. The rage and agony in the creature's dark eyes made Max's heart clench.

Sorry! This is going to hurt!

Max turned his robot's spade arm side on, then jabbed it towards Hydror's tail. At the last moment he twisted the spade, using the edge to prise Hydror's tail armour free.

Max held fast to his robot-suit's juddering

levers, while everything trembled and shook. He felt the suit jerk, and caught sight of Hydror pulling free. The great beast shot past him.

BOOM! Hydror's tail struck the mining suit from behind. Max shot forwards, losing his grip, tumbling out of his seat and through the broken cockpit window.

He pumped his arms and legs, turning in

the water, then his heart gave a painful jolt. Hydror was dead ahead, watching him, dark eyes wild. Beyond the Robobeast, Max could see his mining suit, floating aimlessly, out of reach.

Or perhaps not…

"Activate remote control mode!" he shouted.

A tiny red light inside the shattered cockpit blinked. Hydror opened his huge jaws, then flicked his tail and surged forwards.

Every nerve in Max's body screamed at him to turn and swim for his life. But he knew he couldn't outswim Hydror. He reached out a shaking hand, and closed his fingers in a pincer grip. Behind the leopard seal, the robotic suit did the same, catching the huge creature by the tail again.

Hydror jerked in the water, held tight in the suit's claw. Max kicked back, swimming away from the beast, giving himself space. The robot suit copied his actions, dragging Hydror by the tail. The furious seal flailed and twisted, trying to break free. Max lifted his other hand, trying to hold it steady, reaching forwards. The suit's spade arm inched closer to the helmet on Hydror's head.

"Max!" Lia called.

The Merryn girl and Max's mother were swimming towards Hydror on the back of Lia's squid. They stopped alongside Max's robot suit behind the furious seal.

"I don't know how long I can do it for, but I'll try to calm the seal."

Lia put her fingertips to her temples, using her Aqua Powers. Gradually, Hydror's frantic motion slowed. The seal stopped bucking, and instead stared at Max with a look of cold, hard fury.

"I need to get back in the mining suit,"

said Max. "It's too dangerous to use the remote sensor. One sneeze and I might blind Hydror."

Lia was clenching her eyes shut, focused on keeping the seal calm. "Do it," she murmured.

"Deactivate sensor," Max said. The mining suit's robotic claw opened, releasing the Robobeast. Now, only Lia's Aqua Powers were keeping it from swallowing Max whole. Max swam slowly towards the suit. Hydror's eyes were locked on him, pupils dilated with fury.

Easy, Hydror... Stay calm... Max edged into the cockpit, taking up the controls. Carefully, he moved two levers, sliding the spade hand under the edge of the helmet. *Here goes!* He eased the helmet off, dragging with it the breathing gear – like a plaster ripped from a wound. Hydror shook its colossal head and gazed at Max. All the rage and hatred in the seal's dark eyes had vanished.

Lia let her hands fall and smiled. "Hydror's free!"

The muscular animal lunged towards Max…

Max flinched, but felt a whoosh of water

over his face as the seal soared over him. Then the creature shot up to the surface, snatched a breath of air, flicked its long front flippers and swam away.

Lia let out a long satisfied sigh, watching it go. Niobe smiled. Max kicked from the robot suit's cockpit and swam to their side.

"Thank you, Ginni!" Lia said, running her hand along the squid's flank.

She and Niobe slid from Ginni's back. The squid's huge, silvery eye gazed at Lia for a moment, then Ginni pulsed away.

Together, Max, Lia and Niobe headed up to the surface, aiming for the cluster of scientists and guards treading water nearby.

Max thrust his head out into sunlight and shook the water from his hair. Niobe and Lia bobbed up beside him.

"Good job, Max!" Niobe said.

Max grinned, and arched an eyebrow at

Lia. "See, I told you the robot suit would come in useful!" he said.

Lia rolled her eyes, but then smiled. "Okay," she said. "I admit taking on the seal like that was pretty cool." She frowned suddenly. "Hey! No you don't!"

Max followed her gaze, to see Lieutenant Jared silently breaking away from the group, swimming with a steady breaststroke. The water around him rippled and Rivet's shiny head broke the surface. The dogbot grabbed Jared's lapel in his teeth, and started to drag the lieutenant back.

"Get off!" Jared shouted, swatting at Rivet's metal head.

You'd think he'd learn! Max thought, watching the lieutenant wince with pain.

Rivet paddled on, pulling Jared through the water like a ragdoll.

"Got nasty man, Max!" Rivet barked.

"Good boy, Rivet!" Lia said.

Dr Shah swam over to join Niobe, Lia and Max. She smiled broadly and pointed.

"The Aquoran troops have arrived," she said. "I can't thank you all enough. You saved our lives."

Max turned to see a fleet of naval ships sailing towards them, headed by his father's vessel.

Max grinned. "All in a day's work, he said."

His earpiece crackled, and Callum's familiar voice came through. "We picked up your distress signal from Quantium-5," Callum said. "What's going on out here, Max?"

"Dad!" Max said. "Everyone's safe…" Max's voice faltered as he thought of Leos. "Well, almost everyone," he said.

"Everyone that matters!" Lia cut in.

"What do you mean?" Callum asked.

"It's a long story," Niobe said, suddenly looking tired. "I'm sure Max and Lia will explain everything on the way back, while I take a long hot shower and a well-earned rest. Otherwise, I can't promise Lieutenant Jared will make it back to Aquora in one piece."

Max heard his father splutter and cough with surprise. "This sounds like it's going to be quite a story!" Callum said.

Max and Lia exchanged a grin.

"That's one way of putting it," Max said.

Max heard a trumpeting call. In the distance, he saw the huge leopard seal leap above the surface, before splashing back beneath the waves. Max was proud that he had helped free another ocean creature from robotics. But then a dark thought entered his mind, and he sighed.

"What's wrong?" asked Lia.

Max shook his head. "There might be others in Aquora who knew about Hydror."

Niobe nodded grimly. "We'll carry out a full investigation when we're back. We'll make sure nothing like this ever happens again."

Max smiled, feeling better. He saw his father clamber out of the hatch of his submarine. Max waved at him. Then he glanced round

at Lia and his mum. He knew that whatever threat they faced in the future, they would meet it together.

THE END

Don't miss this exciting Sea Quest book,
in which Max faces

GORT
THE DEADLY SNATCHER

Read on for a sneak preview!

CHAPTER ONE

PEACE

Max's stomach fizzed with excitement as he swam through clear waters, making one final check on his father's latest construction. It was a giant, air-filled plexiglass dome, right at the heart of the Merryn city of Sumara. Max ran his eyes slowly over each hexagonal panel, looking for cracks, or the slightest trickle of bubbles. Through the plexiglass, he could see black-clad Aquoran technicians scurrying about like insects inside the dome.

"No holes, Max!" Rivet, Max's dogbot barked from just ahead.

"Just as well!" Lia said. The Merryn princess frowned at the giant structure from the back of her swordfish, Spike. "I can't believe our guests are about to arrive and we're still checking for leaks!"

Max grinned. "Dad's just being extra cautious. We've been all over the dome a hundred times. And it's made using the latest tech!"

"Hmm," Lia said, "maybe that's what's worrying me." Then she smiled. "Anyway, I can't wait for the ceremony to start!" Max felt a swell of pride as he ran his eyes over the dome. Without his father's technical skills, Sumara's first deep-sea peace conference would never have been possible.

The sound of chatter and laughter drifted up to them along with the salty tang of seaweed cakes and festive treats.

Max turned away from the dome and gazed down over Sumara's broad main street, Treaty Avenue. The wide street ran from Treaty Square, straight through the

dome, then out the other side, and on to Lia's father's palace. Glowing spheres mounted on coral pillars bathed the avenue in silver light. Merryn of all ages lined the approach to the dome, pressed tightly together, wearing their best beaded tunics. Max could see children and babies on their parents' shoulders waving bright flags.

"It looks like everyone in Sumara's turned

out to greet their guests!" Max said.

Lia nodded. "And we couldn't have hoped for better weather." The current stirred her long silver hair, making it shimmer in the soft glow filtering from the dome. The water was crystal clear, with no silt to muddy the view of the surrounding coral towers of Sumara.

"True," Max said. "Which means they should be on time." He lifted his eyes to scan the ocean beyond the city. "In fact – I think that's the first of them arriving now!"

A narrow submarine barge, faceted to shine like a diamond, was gliding slowly towards Sumara, reflecting the lights and colours of the underwater city.

"Pretty boat, Max!" Rivet barked. A chorus of cheers went up from the crowd as the gleaming barge reached Treaty Avenue, then inched towards the docks on the side of the dome.

COLLECT THEM ALL!

SERIES 8:

THE KING OF ILLUSION

978 1 40834 090 5

978 1 40834 099 8

978 1 40834 093 6

978 1 40834 095 0

DISCOVER THE FIRST SERIES OF SEA QUEST:

978 1 40831 848 5

978 1 40831 849 2

978 1 40831 850 8

978 1 40831 851 5

WIN AN EXCLUSIVE GOODY BAG

In every Sea Quest book the Sea Quest logo is hidden in one of the pictures. Find the logo in this book, make a note of which page it appears on and go online to enter the competition at

www.seaquestbooks.co.uk

We will be picking five lucky winners to win some special Sea Quest goodies.

You can also send your entry on a postcard to:

Sea Quest Competition,
Orchard Books, Carmelite House
50 Victoria Embankment
London EC4Y 0DZ

Don't forget to include your name and address!

GOOD LUCK

Closing Date: 31st December 2016

DARE YOU DIVE IN?

Deep in the water lurks a new breed of Beast.

If you want the latest news and exclusive Sea Quest goodies, join our Sea Quest Club!

Visit www.seaquestbooks.co.uk/club and sign up today!

DON'T MISS THE
BRAND NEW SERIES OF:

Series 18: THE TRIAL OF HEROES

KRYTOR
THE BLOOD BAT

978 1 40834 086 8

SOARA
THE STINGING SPECTRE

978 1 40834 088 2

DROGAN
THE JUNGLE MENACE

978 1 40834 295 4

KARIXA
THE DIAMOND WARRIOR

978 1 40834 309 8

IF YOU LIKE SEA QUEST, YOU'LL LOVE BEAST QUEST!

Series 1: COLLECT THEM ALL!

An evil wizard has enchanted the magical Beasts of Avantia. Only a true hero can free the Beasts and save the land. Is Tom the hero Avantia has been waiting for?

FERNO
THE FIRE DRAGON
978 1 84616 483 5

SEPRON
THE SEA SERPENT
978 1 84616 482 8

ARCTA
THE MOUNTAIN GIANT
978 1 84616 484 2

TAGUS
THE HORSE MAN
978 1 84616 486 6

NANOOK
THE SNOW MONSTER
978 1 84616 485 9

EPOS
THE FLAME BIRD
978 1 84616 487 3